Thunder and Lightning

A Level One Reader

By Alice K. Flanagan

The Child's World®

See the lightning flash.

Lightning is a stream of light rushing through the air.

Lightning strikes the air or the ground.

Lightning can also strike inside a cloud or between clouds.

8

Lightning gives off heat. When it cools, it makes a loud sound called thunder.

You see lightning before you hear thunder. That's because light moves faster than sound.

If lightning hits the ground, it can cause a fire.

In a lightning storm, keep away from tall trees and telephone poles.

Stay out of water during a storm.

Never get too close to lightning!

Word List

flash

heat

lightning

storm

strikes

telephone poles

thunder

Note to Parents and Educators

Welcome to Wonder Books®! These books provide text at three different levels for beginning readers to practice and strengthen their reading skills. Additionally, the use of nonfiction text provides readers the valuable opportunity to *read to learn*, not just to learn to read.

These leveled readers allow children to choose books at their level of reading confidence and performance. Nonfiction Level One books offer beginning readers simple language, word choice, and sentence structure as well as a word list. Nonfiction Level Two books feature slightly more difficult vocabulary, longer sentences, and longer total text. In the back of each Nonfiction Level Two book are an index and a list of books and Web sites for finding out more information. Nonfiction Level Three books continue to extend word choice and length of text. In the back of each Nonfiction Level Three book are a glossary, an index, and a list of books and Web sites for further research.

State and national standards in reading and language arts emphasize using nonfiction at all levels of reading development. Wonder Books® fill the historical void in nonfiction material for the primary grade readers with the additional benefit of a leveled text.

About the Author

Alice K. Flanagan taught elementary school for ten years. Now she writes for children and teachers. She has been writing for more than twenty years. Some of her books include biographies, phonics books, holiday books, and information books about careers, animals, and weather. Alice K. Flanagan lives with her husband in Chicago, Illinois.

Published by The Child's World®
P.O. Box 326
Chanhassen, MN 55317-0326
800-599-READ
www.childsworld.com

Photo Credits
© A & J Verkaik/CORBIS: 6, 9
© Benjamin Shearn/Taxi: 5
© Byron Aughenbaug/The Image Bank: 10
© Charles W. Campbell/CORBIS: 13
© Dale O'Dell/CORBIS: 21
© Dugald Bremner/Tony Stone: 17
© Joel Sartore/National Geographic: 2
© Raymond Gehman/CORBIS: 14
© Rod Currie/Tony Stone: 18
© Steve Bloom/Taxi: cover

Editorial Directions, Inc.: E. Russell Primm and Emily J. Dolbear, Editors;
Alice K. Flanagan, Photo Research; Emily J. Dolbear, Photo Selector

The Child's World®: Mary Berendes, Publishing Director

Library of Congress Cataloging-in-Publication Data
Flanagan, Alice K.
Thunder and lightning / by Alice K. Flanagan.
    p. cm. — (Wonder books series. A level one reader)
Summary: Simple text describes thunder and lightning, what causes these
phenomena, and what they can do to the Earth.
Includes bibliographical references and index.
  ISBN 1-56766-451-2 (lib bdg. : alk. paper)
 1. Thunder—Juvenile literature. 2. Lightning—Juvenile literature.
[1. Thunder. 2. Lightning.] I. Title. II. Series: Wonder books
(Chanhassen, Minn.)
  QC968.2 .F56 2003
  551.56'32—dc21
                              2002151610